T0356893

OUTSIDE

Outside

SIX SHORT STORIES BY BARRY LOPEZ

Introduction by James Perrin Warren

Afterword by the Author

Engravings by Barry Moser

TRINITY UNIVERSITY PRESS & SAN ANTONIO

INTRODUCTION

THE STORYTELLER

Barry Lopez has been publishing short stories and essays in distinguished literary magazines for nearly forty years. The relationship between landscape and the imagination is a central concern in his work, as is the role of storytelling in bringing communities into healthy relations with the land. The essay "Landscape and Narrative" (1984) resonates deeply with the aims and methods of the stories in *Outside.* The essay opens with a gathering of hunters in Anaktuvuk Pass, in the Brooks Range of Alaska. Lopez sits among a group of men listening to hunting stories, and he is particularly taken with the stories of wolverines. One man's story of an astonishing encounter between a hunter on a snow machine and an intelligent wolverine dominates the opening, but the effect of the wolverine stories on the group of listeners is even more astonishing: "The landscape seemed alive because of the stories. It was precisely these ocherous tones, this kind of willow, exactly this austerity that had informed the wolverine narratives." The stories make the landscape come alive because they have truthfully evoked the landscape in its particulars. That is the physical landscape, which Lopez calls the "external landscape" or "exterior landscape" in the essay. Another landscape is the "internal" or "interior" one, and it might be called a spiritual landscape or mental landscape. For Lopez, as for traditional indigenous storytellers, the truth of the story and the value of the storyteller rest in the unimpeachable authority and integrity of the external landscape, which the Navajo say exhibits a "sacred order." If the story is successful, it brings the external landscape and the internal landscape into harmony, creating a sense of well-being in the listener and healing any disharmonies in the internal landscape. For Lopez, storytelling connects directly to spiritual rituals and ceremonies of traditional indigenous people, and the qualities of storytelling he values most focus on the role of the storyteller in forging a healthy community living in a healthy landscape.

The six stories gathered here show the growth of a storyteller. The collections *Desert Notes* (1976) and *River Notes* (1979) are closely linked to one another, and they give us a strong sense of Lopez as a young writer, since many of the stories date from the early to mid-1970s. *Field Notes* (1994), closer in chronology and form to the collection *Winter Count* (1981), is the work of an accomplished writer of prize-winning fiction and nonfiction. Even as a young writer, however, Lopez clearly avoids the role of the romantic, isolated artist. His contact with indigenous storytellers reinforces his sense of the writer as serving the cultural memory of a community, reminding us how to live a decent life, how to behave properly toward other people and toward the land. The name he provides for this figure of the storyteller in *Arctic Dreams* (1986) is "*isumataq* . . . a person who can create the atmosphere in which wisdom shows itself."

Wisdom is not owned by any person or culture or language. In defining its outlines in *Arctic Dreams*, Lopez imagines a scene in which such wisdom might show itself. "I could easily imagine some Thomas Merton–like person, the estimable rather than the famous people of our age, sitting with one or two Eskimo men and women in a coastal village, corroborating the existence of this human wisdom in yet another region of the world, and looking around to the mountains, the ice, the birds to see what makes it possible to put it into words." The figures in Lopez's imagined scene form in effect a group of estimable storytellers from different cultures and traditions. Their goal is first to bind their human wisdom into the land with words and, second, to use their words to bind their human communities together with the land. Storytelling embodies, then, a conversation with the land, and in its most elevated and authentic form it combines the empirical, aesthetic, and spiritual landscapes.

Like the Inuit *isumataq*, Thomas Merton (1915–1968) figures the wisdom that shows itself through storytelling. Lopez considered becoming a Trappist monk and in November 1966 stayed at the abbey of Gethsemani in Kentucky, Merton's monastic home. He was especially attracted to the combination of physical labor and spirituality, to the contemplative life. For Lopez as a young man, the contemplative life involves the risky decision to become a professional writer. It is with a sense of vocation, then, that Lopez quotes Merton's *The Wisdom of the Desert* (1960) near the beginning of *Desert Notes*: "With the Desert Fathers you have the characteristic of a clean break with a conventional, accepted social context in order to swim for one's life into an apparently irrational void."

The stories in *Outside* break from convention with a great enthusiasm for experimentation. The first-person narrators are so persuasive that readers are sometimes fooled into thinking that they represent Lopez himself. The early fictions do not employ conventional characterization, action, plot, conflict, or resolution. The narrators of "Desert Notes," "The Search for the Heron," and "Within Birds' Hearing" resemble one another in their physical and spiritual journeys across the landscape. They encounter animals, sometimes in extraordinary ways that may recall the wolverine in "Landscape and Narrative." They place their faith in the landscape, in what the landscape can teach them, in the beauty and wonder of the land. They are often solitary, isolated from any social context, but they are not alone.

In the other three stories, the first-person narrators focus on human communities, both in their weakness and in their potential strength. "Twilight" begins and ends with the narrator seated upon a "storm pattern rug woven out of the mind of a Navajo woman, Ahlnsaha." The first half of the story details the numerous owners of the rug from 1934 to 1966, each of whom becomes progressively less certain—or truthful—about the tribal origin of the art or what its proper function should be. The second half of the story evokes, in present tense, the narrator's visions as he sits on the rug at twilight, "the best time to see what is happening." In contrast to the lies told by

8

salespeople in the first part of the story, the narrator's fleeting visions deliver momentary truths. The visions mix images of nature and culture as the narrator works through the senses of sight, hearing, and smell. The visions deliver an ambiguous sense of truth—sometimes promising much, sometimes little. In hearing the flight of the gray eagle over the desert, however, the listener becomes exquisitely intimate with the landscape. In creating that sense of intimacy in the reader, Lopez works powerfully on a personal level and creates yet another sense of intimacy.

By such writing, we come to accept that magical transformations join human beings to the landscape and to one another. The narrator of "The Falls" accepts as fact that his unnamed friend is a shamanistic shape-shifter who can become part of the landscape. The narrator's intimacy with his friend allows him to tell of the man's vision quest in the Crazy Mountains as if he were himself part of the man's journey. The man visits the narrator occasionally, at ten-year intervals, but even when the narrator misses a visit he can sense his friend's presence. At the climax of these repeated visits, the narrator witnesses the man's leap from the falls, and he implies that the man becomes a salmon as he dives into the water.

Clearly, Lopez's narrators bear witness to extraordinary patterns and purposes. They must listen attentively to what their story must become. Those are the elevated demands placed on Marlis Damien, the narrator of "Empira's Tapestry." Impressed by Marlis's storytelling, Empira gives Marlis the storyteller's stick from Ghana, appointing her the witness of Empira's life and art. By telling her story truthfully, Marlis gathers the threads of Empira's tapestry, showing that she understands Empira's admirable strength and integrity.

By such gatherings, individuals and communities can flourish. The storyteller is vital to the community and to a healthy landscape, but the vital relationship is also reciprocal. Barry Lopez shows his gifts as a storyteller. And by such gatherings as this one, we show our reverence for estimable lives and places. In those ways, we participate, along with Lopez, in the long history of storytelling. We become part of the atmosphere in which wisdom shows itself.

—JAMES PERRIN WARREN

Outside

SIX SHORT STORIES BY BARRY LOPEZ

In the early 1950s, when people living in the Los Angeles Basin
spoke of going away for the weekend, often east over the
mountains to the Mojave Desert, they would say that
they were going "to go outside."

g

DESERT NOTES

DESERT NOTES

I KNOW YOU ARE TIRED. I am tired too. Will you walk along the edge of the desert with me? I would like to show you what lies before us.

All my life I have wanted to trick blood from a rock. I have dreamed about raising the devil and cutting him in half. I have thought too about never being afraid of anything at all. This is where you come to do those things.

I know what they tell you about the desert but you mustn't believe them. This is no deathbed. Dig down, the earth is moist. Boulders have turned to dust here, the dust feels like graphite. You can hear a man breathe at a distance of twenty yards. You can see out there to the edge where the desert stops and the mountains begin. You think it is perhaps ten miles. It is more than a hundred. Just before the sun sets all the colors will change. Green will turn to blue, red to gold.

16

I've been told there is very little time left, that we must get all these things about time and place straight. If we don't, we will only have passed on and have changed nothing. That is why we are here I think, to change things. It is why I came to the desert.

Here things are sharp, elemental. There's no one to look over your shoulder to find out what you're doing with your hands, or to ask if you have considered the number of people dying daily of malnutrition. If you've been listening you must suspect that a knife will be very useful out here—not to use, just to look at.

There is something else here, too, even more important: explanations will occur to you, seeming to clarify; but they can be a kind of trick. You will think you have hold of the idea when you only have hold of its clothing.

Feel how still it is. You can become impatient here, willing to accept any explanation in order to move on. This appears to be nothing at all, but it is a wall between you and what you are after. Be sure you are not tricked into thinking there is nothing to fear. Moving on is not important. You must wait. You must take things down to the core. You must be careful with everything, even with what I tell you.

This is how to do it. Wait for everything to get undressed and go to sleep. Forget to explain to yourself why you are here. Listen attentively. Just before dawn you will finally hear faint music. This is the sound of the loudest dreaming, the dreams of boulders. Continue to listen until the music isn't there. What you thought about boulders will evaporate and what you know will become clear. Each night it will be harder. Listen until you can hear the dreams of the dust that settles on your head.

I must tell you something else. I have waited out here for rattlesnakes. They never come. The moment eludes me and I hate it. But it keeps me out here. I would like to trick the rattlesnake into killing itself. I would like this kind of finality. I would like to begin again with the snake. If such a thing were possible. The desert would be safe. You could stay here forever.

I will give you a few things: bits of rock, a few twigs, this shell of a beetle blown out here by the wind. You should try to put the bits of rock back together to form a stone, although I cannot say that all these pieces are from the same stone. If they don't fit together look for others that do. You should try to coax some leaves from these twigs. You will first have

18

to determine whether they are alive or dead. And you will have to find out what happened to the rest of the beetle, the innards. When you have done these things you will know a little more than you did before. But be careful. It will occur to you that these tasks are silly or easily done. This is a sign, the first one, that you are being fooled.

I hope you won't be here long. After you have finished with the stone, the twigs and the beetle, other things will suggest themselves, and you must take care of them. I see you are already tired. But you must stay. This is the pain of it all. You can't keep leaving.

Do you hear how silent it is? This will be a comfort as you work. Do not laugh. When I first came here I laughed very loud and the sun struck me across the face and it took me a week to recover. You will only lose time by laughing.

I will leave you alone to look out on the desert. What makes you want to leave now is what is trying to kill you. Have the patience to wait until the rattlesnake kills itself. Others may tell you that this has already happened, and this may be true. But wait until you see for yourself, until you are sure.

TWILIGHT

TWILIGHT

I AM SITTING ON a storm pattern rug woven out of the mind of a Navajo woman, Ahlnsaha, and traded to a man named Dobrey in Winslow, Arizona, for groceries in August 1934.

In the fall of 1936 a Swedish farmer, Kester Vorland, his land gone out from under him in the Depression, leaves his wife and three children in the car and, picking his moment perfectly, steps back into the store to steal the rug while Dobrey is busy in the back with a broken saddle. He trades it the next day in Flagstaff for groceries and $25 cash and moves on to Needles. It is bought later by a young man named Diego Martin who takes it back to San Bernardino, California, with him. He boasts of it to his friends, a piece of shrewd buying. When he is married in 1941 he gives it to his wife and, one flat September night, they make love on it, leaving a small stain that the girl, Yonella, can easily point out but which Diego will not believe, even when she shows him. He believes it is a stain left by an insect; he forbids her to show the rug to anyone after this. He dies in a bar fight in Honolulu on April 16, 1943, a corporal in the Marines. Yonella sells everything. An old woman with red hair and liver spots on her throat pouch named Elizabeth Reiner buys the rug for $45 and takes it home with her to Santa Barbara. In 1951 her daughter comes to visit and her grandson John Charles who is ten begins to covet the rug; when the mother and daughter fall into an argument over something, the older woman angrily gives it to the boy (she snatches it down off the wall), a demonstration of her generosity. She later tells her daughter not to come back again and begins to miss the rug and feel foolish. The boy doesn't care. He vows he will always write her at Christmastime, even if his mother forbids it.

On the train from Los Angeles to Prairie du Chien the boy keeps himself wrapped in the rug like a turtle. He sits on the bed in his underwear with it over his shoulders and watches Nebraska. When he is sixteen John Charles falls in love with Dolores Patherway who is nineteen and a whore. One night she trades him twenty-five minutes for the blanket, but he does not see it this way: it is a gift, the best he can offer, a thing of power. That night she is able to sell it to a Great

Lakes sailor for $60. She tells him it is genuine Sioux, there at the battle of the Little Big Horn, and will always bring a good price. The sailor's name is Benedict Langer, from a good Catholic family in Ramapo, New Jersey, and he has never had hard liquor or even VD but in three weeks in the service his father said would make a man of him he has lain in confusion with six different women who have told him he was terrific; he has sensed a pit opening. The day after he buys it Benedict gives the blanket to a friend, Frank Winter, and goes to look for a priest in Green Bay, the football town. In March 1959 Frank mails it to his parents for an anniversary present (it has been in his footlocker for eighteen months and smells like mothballs, a condition he remedies by airing it at night from the signal deck of the USS *Kissell*). He includes with it a document he has had made up in the ship's print shop to the effect that it is an authentic Pawnee blanket, so his parents will be proud, can put it up on the wall of their retirement home in Boca Raton, Florida, next to the maracas from Guadalajara. They leave it in the box in the hall closet; they do not talk about it. Mr. Winter confides to his wife in the dark one night that he doesn't believe in the powers of medicine men.

On July 17, 1963, Frank Winter dies instantly when his foot hits a land mine in the Mekong Delta. His father waits a month before donating the blanket and the boy's other belongings to Catholic Charities. Father Peter Donnell, a local priest, a man of some sensitivity, lays the rug down on brown wall-to-wall carpeting in the foyer of the refectory of the Catholic Church in Boca Raton, arranging two chairs and a small table precisely on it (he likes especially the Ganado red color) before the Monsignor asks him to remove it. Father Donnell keeps the rug in his room, spread out flat under his mattress for a year. He takes it with him when he is transferred to Ames, Iowa, where it is finally bought in an Easter bazaar as Father Donnell endures a self-inflicted purging of personal possessions. It is bought by antique dealers, Mr. and Mrs. Theodore Wishton Spanner of Jordan Valley, Oregon (as they sign the register). The following winter I buy it from Mrs. Spanner who tells me the rug has been woven by a Comanche who learned his craft from a Navajo, that she bought it on the reservation in Oklahoma. It is certified. I take the rug home and at dusk I undress and lie down under it so that it completely covers my body. I listen all night. I do not hear anything. But in this time I am

able to sort out all the smells buried in the threads and the
sounds still reverberating deep in the fibers. It is what I have
been looking for.

It is this rug I have carefully spread out now, east and west
over the dust. It is only from such a height above the floor
of the desert that one is able to see clearly what is going on.

The moon has just risen; the sun has just gone down.
There are only a few stars up and a breeze is blowing in from
the south. The air smells like wet cottonwood leaves.

This is the best time to see what is happening. Everyone
who is passing through will be visible for a short time. Already
I have seen the priest with his Bible bound in wolves' fur and
the blackbirds asleep in his hair.

I see the woman who smells like sagebrush and her three
children with the large white eyes and tattered leggings. I see
the boy who rolls in dust like a horse and the legionnaire
with the alabaster skin polished smooth by the wind. I see
the magnificent jethery loping across the desert like a grey-
hound with his arms full of oars. I watch cheetahs in silver
chariots pulled by a span of white crows. I see the rainbow in
arabesques of the wind.

The night gets deeper. I pull down to listen for Ahlnsaha:
she is crying in Arizona. This is what she is singing:

> Go to the white rain
> Ta ta ta ta
> Go to the white rain
> Ta ta ta ta
> I see the horses
> Ta ta ta ta
> They are feeding above there.

There is no rain; there are no horses. Her music falls into
pieces with her tears in the dust like lies. She smells like your
face in wheat.

The moon is up higher, clearing the thin clouds on the
horizon.

The two girls with the sun in a spiderweb bag are standing by the mountains south talking with the blue snake that
makes holes in the wind with his whistle.

I can smell the heat of the day stuck on the edges of the
cracks in the earth like a salt crust after a tide. I lay back and
watch the sky. I close my eyes. I run my hands out smooth over

the rug and feel the cold rising from the earth. When I come again I will bring a friar's robe with a deep cowl and shoes of jute fiber. I will run like a madman to the west all night until I begin to fall asleep; then I will walk back, being careful to correct for the tilt of the earth, the force of Coriolis, reading my breviary by the precise arrowlight of stars, assured of my destination.

The spent day hugs the desert floor like a fallen warrior. I am warm. I am alert for any sort of light. I believe there is someplace out there where you can see right down into the heart of the earth. The light there is strong enough to burn out your eyes like sap in a fire. But I won't go near it. I let it pass. I like to know that if I need it, with only a shovel or a small spade, I can begin digging and recall the day.

This time is the only time you will see the turtles massed on the eastern border for the march to the western edge where there is water, and then back the same night to hide in the bushes and smash insects dazed to lethargy in the cold. I have spoken with these turtles. They are reticent about their commitments. Each one looks like half the earth.

This is the only time you can study both of your shadows. If you sit perfectly still and watch your primary shadow as the sun sets you will be able to hold it long enough to see your other shadow fill up when the moon rises like a porcelain basin with clear water. If you turn carefully to face the south you may regard both of them: to understand the nature of silence you must be able to see into this space between your shadows.

This is the only time you will be able to smell water and not mistake it for the smell of a sheet of granite, or confuse it with the smell of marble or darkness. If you are moving about at this lime, able to go anywhere you choose, you will find water as easily as if you were looking for your hands. It may take you some hours, even days to arrive at the place, but there will be no mistake about the direction to go once you smell it. The smell of water is not affected by the air currents so you won't need to know the direction of the wind; the smell of water lays along the surface of the earth like a long stick of peeled elmwood.

This is the only time you can hear the flight of the gray eagle over the desert. You cannot see him because he fades with the sun and is born out of it in the morning but it is possible to hear his wings pumping against the columns of warm air rising and hear the slip of the wind in his feathers as he tilts his gyre out over the desert floor. There is nothing out there for him, no rabbits to hunt, no cliff faces to fall from,

no rock on which to roost, but he is always out there at this time fading to gray and then to nothing, turning on the wind with his eyes closed. It doesn't matter how high he goes or how far away he drifts, you will be able to hear him. It is only necessary to lie out flat somewhere and listen for the sound, like the wrinkling of the ocean.

The last thing you will notice will be the stones, small bits of volcanic ash, black glass, blue tourmaline, sapphires, narrow slabs of gray feldspar, rose quartz, sheets of mica and blood agate. They are small enough to be missed, laying down in the cracks of the desert floor, but they are the last things to give up the light; you will see them flare and burn like coals before they let go.

It is good to have a few of these kinds of stones with you in a pocket or cupped in your hand before you go to sleep. One man I knew, only for a short time, was sure the stones were more important than anything else; he kept a blue one tied behind his ear. One evening while we were talking he reached over and with a wet finger took alkaline dust and painted a small lightning bolt on his right cheek. I regarded him for more than an hour before it became too dark to see. I rolled myself up in this blanket and slept.

THE SEARCH FOR THE HERON

THE SEARCH FOR THE HERON

I SEE YOU ON THE FAR SIDE of the river, standing at the edge of familiar shadows, before a terrified chorus of young alders on the bank. I do not think you know it is raining. You are oblivious to the *thuck* of drops rolling off the tube of your neck and the slope of your back. (Above, in the sweepy cedars, drops pool at the tips of leather needles, break away, are sheered by the breeze and, *thuck*, hit the hollow-boned, crimson-colored shoulders of the bird and fall swooning into the river.)

Perhaps you know it is raining. The intensity of your stare is then not oblivion, only an effort to spot between the rain splashes in the river (past your feet, so well-known, there beneath the hammered surface, like twigs in the pebbles) the movement of a trout.

I know: your way is to be inscrutable. When pressed you leave. This is no more unexpected or mysterious than that you give birth to shadows. Or silence. I watch from a distance.

With respect. I think of standing beside you when you have
died of your own brooding over the water—as shaken as I
would be at the collapse of a cathedral, wincing deep inside
as at the screech of an overloaded cart.

You carry attribution well, refusing to speak. With your
warrior's feathers downsloped at the back of your head, those
white sheaves formed like a shield overlaying your breast,
your gray-blue cast, the dark tail feathers—do you wear
wolves' tails about your ankles and dance in clearings in the
woods when your blood is running? I wonder where you
have fought warrior. Where!

You retreat beneath your cowl, spread wings, rise, drift
upriver as silent as winter trees.

I follow you. You have caught me with your reticence. I
will listen to whatever they say about you, what anyone who
has seen you wishes to offer—and I will return to call across
the river to you, to confirm or deny. If you will not speak I
will have to consider making you up.

Your sigh, I am told, is like the sound of rain driven against
tower bells. You smell like wild ginger. When you lift your
foot from the river, water doesn't run off it to spoil the transparent surface of the shallows. The water hesitates to offend

you. You stare down with that great yellow eye, I am told, like some prehistoric rattlesnake: that dangerous, that blinding in your strike, that hate-ridden. But (someone else has insisted) you really do smell like wild ginger, and snakes smell like cucumbers. A false lead.

Cottonwoods along the river, stained with your white excrement, are young enough to volunteer complaint about you. They have grown so fast and so high with such little effort that they can understand neither failure nor triumph. So they will say anything they think might be to their advantage. I, after a somewhat more difficult life, am aware that they will lie, and that lies serve in their way.

(It was one of these who told me you were without mercy and snakelike.) One of them said something about your fishy breath—vulgar talk, I know. But I heard it out. It is, after all, in their branches where you have dreamed at night, as immobile as a piece of lumber left in their limbs, and considered your interior life. This idea attracts me. I know: this is not something to inquire into with impunity, but I did not start out on this to please you. And in spite of my impatience I am respectful.

One dream alone reveals your grief. The trees said you dreamed most often of the wind. You dreamed that you lived somewhere with the wind, with the wind rippling your feathers; and that children were born of this, that they are the movement of water in all the rivers. You wade, it is suggested, among your children, staring hard, pecking in that lightning way your life from the water that is your child; and sleeping in trees that do not hold you sacred.

I know why you appear so fierce and self-contained. I can imagine fear in the form of a frog in your beak screaming and you, undisturbed, cool. When you finally speak up, feigning ignorance with me won't do; enigmatic locutions, distracting stories of the origin of the universe—these will not do. I expect the wisdom of the desert out of you.

The cottonwoods also told me of a dance, that you dreamed of a dance: more than a hundred great blue herons riveted by the light of dawn, standing with wind-ruffled feathers on broad slabs of speckled gray granite, river-washed bedrock, in that sharp, etching backlight, their sleek bills glinting, begin to lift their feet from the thin sheet of water and to put them back down. The sound of the rhythmic splash, the delicate *kersplash* of hundreds of feet, came up in the sound of the river and so at first was lost; but the shards of water, caught, blinding in the cutting light (now the voices, rising, a keening) began to form a mist in which appeared rainbows against the white soft breasts; and where drops of water dolloped like beads of mercury on the blue–gray feathers, small rainbows of light here; and in the eyes (as the voices, louder, gathering on one, high, trembling note) rainbows—the birds cradled in light shattered in rainbows everywhere, and with your great blue wings fanning that brilliant mist, open, utterly vulnerable and stunning, you urged them to begin to revolve in the light, stretching their wings, and you lay back your head and closed the steely eyes and from deep within your belly came the roar of a cataract, like the howling of wolves—that long moment of your mournful voice. The birds quieted, their voices quieted. The water quieted, it quieted, until there was only your quivering voice, the sound of the birth of rivers, tapering finally to silence, to the sound of dawn, the birds standing there full of grace. One or two feathers floating on the water.

I understand it is insensitive to inquire further, but you see now your silence becomes even more haunting.

I believe we will dance together someday. Before then will I have to have been a trout, bear scars from your stabbing misses and so have some deeper knowledge? Then will we dance? I cannot believe it is so far between knowing what must be done and doing it.

The cottonwoods, these too-young trees, said once, long ago, you had a premonition in a nightmare. An enormous owl arrived while you slept and took your daughter away, pinioned in his gray fists. You woke, bolt upright, in the middle of the night to find her there, undisturbed beside you. You aired your feathers, glared into the moon-stilled space over the water and went uneasily back to sleep. In the morning— your first glance—the limb was empty. You were young, you had also lost a wife, and you went down to the river and tore out your feathers and wept. The soundlessness of it was what you could not get over.

The cottonwoods said there was more, but I put up my hand, tired, on edge at the sound of my own voice asking questions. I went into the trees, wishing to cry, I thought, for what had been lost, feeling how little I knew, how anxious I was, how young.

The big maples, where you have slept since then—I resolved to ask them about your dreams. No; they refused. I climbed up in their limbs, imploring. They were silent. I was angered and made a fool of myself beating on the trunks with my fists screaming, "Tell me about the bird! It is only a bird!"

Learning your dreams unnerved me. What unholy trespass I had made.

When I regained my composure I apologized, touching the maple trunks gently with my fingers. As I departed a wind moved the leaves of a low branch against my face and I was embarrassed, for I was waiting for some sign of understanding. I walked on, alert now to the wind showing here and there in the grass. The wind suddenly spoke of you as of a father. The thoughts were incomplete, hinting at something incomprehensible, ungraspable, but I learned this: you are able to stand in the river in such a way that the wind makes no sound against you. You arrange yourself so that you cast no shadow and you stop breathing for half an hour. The only sound is the faint movement of your blood. You are quiet enough to hear fish swimming toward you.

When I asked, discreetly, whether long ago you might have fought someone, some enemy whose name I might recognize, the wind was suddenly no longer there. From such strength as is in you I suspect an enemy. I have inquired of the stones at the bottom of the river; I have inquired of your other enemy, the pine marten; I have waded silently with your relatives, the bitterns, alert for any remarks. All to no avail.

I have been crippled by my age, by what I have known. As well as by my youth, by what I have yet to learn, in all these inquiries. It has taken me years, which might have been spent (by someone else) seeking something greater, in some other place. I have sought only you. Enough. I wish to know you, and you will not speak.

It is not easy to tell the rest, but I know you have heard it from others. Now I wish you to hear it from me. I took bits of bone from fish you had eaten and pierced my fingers, letting the blood trail away in the current. I slept on what feathers of yours I could find. From a tree felled in a storm I took your nest, climbed with it to a clearing above the river where there was a good view, as much sky as I could comprehend. Bear grass, pentstemon, blue gilia, wild strawberries, Indian paint-brush growing there. Each night for four nights I made a small fire with sticks from the old nest and looked out toward the edge of the shadows it threw. On the last night I had a great dream. You were standing on a desert plain. You were painted blue and you wore a necklace of white salmon vertebrae. Your eyes huge, red. Before you on the dry, gray earth a snake coiled, slowly weaving the air with his head. You spoke about the beginning of the world, that there was going to be no fear in the world, that everything that was afraid would live poorly.

The snake said coldly, weaving, yes, there would be fear, that fear would make everything strong, and lashed out, open-

ing a wound in your shoulder. As fast, you pinned his head to
the ground and said—the calmness in your voice—fear might
come, and it could make people strong, but it would be worth
nothing without compassion. And you released the snake.

I awoke sprawled in bear grass. It was darker than I could ever
remember a night being. I felt the spot on the planet where I
lay, turned away from the sun. My legs ached. I knew how old
I was lying there on the top of the mountain, a fist of cold air
against my breast as some animal, a mouse perhaps, moved
suddenly under my back.

An unpronounceable forgiveness swept over me. I knew
how much had to be given away, how little could ever be
asked. The sound of geese overhead in the darkness just then,
and all that it meant, was enough.

I leap into the jade color of the winter river. I fight the current to reach the rocks, climb up on them and listen for the
sound of your voice. I stand dripping, shivering in my white
nakedness, in the thin dawn light. Waiting. Silent. You begin
to appear at a downriver bend.

THE FALLS

THE FALLS

Someone must see to it that this story is told: you shouldn't think this man just threw his life away.

When he was a boy there was nothing about him to remember. He looked like anything else—like the trees, like other people, like his dog. The dog was part coyote. Sometimes he would change places with his dog. For a week at a time he was the dog and the dog was himself, and it went by unnoticed. It was harder on the dog, but the boy encouraged him and he did well at it. The dog's name was Leaves.

When the boy went to sleep in the hills he would become the wind or a bird flying overhead. It was, again, harder on the dog, running to keep up, but the dog knew the boy would be a man someday and would no longer want to be a bird or the wind, or even a half-breed dog like himself, but himself. Above all, the dog trusted in time.

This is what happened. The boy grew. Visions came to him.

He began to see things. When he was eighteen he dreamed he should go up in the Crazy Mountains north of Big Timber to dream, and he went. He was careful from whom he took rides. Old cars. Old men only. He was old enough to be careful but not to know why.

The dreaming was four days. I do not know what came to him. He told no one. He spoke with no one. While he was up there the dog, Leaves, slept out on some rocks in the Sweetgrass River, where he would not be bothered, and fasted. I came at dawn and then at dusk to look. I could not tell from a distance if he was asleep or dead. Or about the dog. I would only know it was all right because each morning he was in a different position. The fourth morning—I remember this one the best, the sun like fire on the October trees, so many spider webs sunken under the load of dew, the wind in them, as though the trees were breathing—he was gone. I swam out to see about the dog. Wild iris petals there on the green moss. That was a good dog.

The man was back home in two days. He washed in the river near his home.

He got a job down there around Beatty and I didn't see him for two or three years. The next time was in winter. It was the coldest one I had ever been in. Chickadees froze. The river froze all the way across. I never saw that before. I picked him up hitchhiking north. He had on dark cotton pants and a light jacket and lace shoes. With a brown canvas bag and a hat pulled down over his ears and his hands in his pockets. I pulled over right away. He looked sorry as hell.

I took him all the way up north, to my place. He had some antelope meat with him and we ate good. That was the best meat I ever had. We talked. He wanted to know what I was doing for work. I was cutting wood. He was going to go up to British Columbia, Nanaimo, in there, in spring to look for work. That night when we were going to bed I saw his back in the kerosene light. The muscles looked like water coming over his shoulders and going into the bed of his spine. I went over and hugged him.

I woke up the next morning when it was just getting light. I could not hear the sound of the river and the silence frightened me until I remembered. I heard chopping on the ice. I got dressed and went down. The earth was like rock that winter.

He had cut a hole a few feet across, black water boiling up, flowing out on the ice, freezing. He was standing in the hole naked with his head bowed and his arms straight up over his head with his hands open. He had cut his arms with a knife and the red blood was running down them, down his ribs,

slowing in the cold, to the black water. I could see his body
shaking, the muscles starting to go blue-gray over his bones,
the color of the ice. He called out in a voice so strong I sat
down as though his voice had hit me. I had never heard a
cry like that, his arms down and his fists squeezed tight, his
mouth, those large white teeth, his forehead knotted. The cry
was like a bear, not a man sound, like something he was tear-
ing away from inside himself.

The cry went up like a roar and fell away into a trickle,
like creek water over rocks at the end of summer. He was bent
over with his lips near the water. His fist opened. He put water
to his lips four times, and washed the blood off. He leaped out
of that hole like a salmon and ran off west, around the bend,
gone into the trees, very high steps.

I went down to look at the blood on the gray-white ice.

He cut wood with me that winter. He worked hard. When the
trillium bloomed and the varied thrushes came he went north.
I did not see him again for ten years. I was in North Dakota
harvesting wheat, sleeping in the back of my truck (parked
under cottonwoods for the cool air that ran down their trunks
at night like water). One night I heard my name. He was by
the tailgate.

"You got a good spot," he said. "Yeah. That you?"

"Sure."   57

"How you doing?"

"Good. Talk in the morning."

He sounded tired, like he'd been riding all day.

Next morning someone left, too much drinking, and he
got that job, and so we worked three weeks together, clear up
into Saskatchewan, before we turned around and drove home.
When we came through Stanley Basin in Idaho we crossed
over a little bridge where the Salmon River was only a foot
deep, ten feet across. It came across a big meadow, out of some
quaking aspen. "Let's go up there," he said. "I bet that's good
water." We did. We camped up in those aspen and that was
good water. It was sweet like a woman's lips when you are in
love and holding back.

We came home and he stayed with me that winter, too. I
was getting old then and it was good he was around. In the
spring he left. He told me a lot that winter, but I can't say
these things. When he spoke about them it was like the breeze
when you are asleep in the woods: you listen hard, but it is
not easy. It is not your language. He lived in the desert near
antelope one year, by a lake where geese came in the spring.
The geese did not teach him anything, he said, but it was

good to be around them. The water in the lake was so clear when the geese floated they seemed to be suspended, twenty or twenty-five feet off the ground.

The morning he left he took a knife and carefully scraped his whole body. He put some of these small pieces of skin in the water and scattered the rest over the sagebrush.

He went to work then in another town in Nevada somewhere, I forget, in a lumberyard and he was there for a long time, five or six years. He took time off a lot, went into the mountains for a few weeks, a place where he could see the sun come up and go down. Clean out everything bad that had built up.

When he left that place he went to Alaska, around Anchorage somewhere, but couldn't find any work and ended up at Sitka fishing and then went to Matanuska Valley, working on a farm there. All that time he was alone. Once he came down to see me but I was gone. I knew it when I got home. I went down to the river and saw the place where he went into the water. The ground was soft around the rocks. I knew his feet. I am not a man of great power, but I took what I had and gave it to him that time, everything I had. "You keep going," I said. I raised my hands over my head and stepped into the water and shouted it again. "You keep going!" My heart was pounding like a waterfall.

That time after he left he was gone almost ten years again.
I had a dream he was living up on those salmon rivers in the
north. I don't know. Maybe it was a no-account dream. I knew
he never went south.

Last time I saw him he came to my house in the fall. He
came in quiet as air sitting in a canyon. We made dinner early
and at dusk he went out and I followed him because I knew
he wanted me to. He cut twigs from the ash and cottonwood
and alder and I got undressed. He brushed my body with
these bank-growing trees and said I had always been a good
friend. He said this was his last time. We went swimming a
little. There is a good current at that place. It is hard to swim.

Later we went up to the house and ate. He told me a story
about an old woman who tried to keep two husbands and
stories about a man who couldn't sing but went around making people pay to hear him sing anyway. I laughed until I was
tired out and went to bed. I woke up suddenly, at the end
of a dream. It was the same dream I had once before. About
him climbing up a waterfall out of the sky. I went to look in
his bed. He was gone. I got dressed and drove my truck to
the falls below the willow flats where I killed my first deer
many years ago. 1 ran into the trees, fighting the vine maple

and deadfalls, running now as hard as I could for the river. The thunder of that falls was all around me and the ground shaking. I came out on the river, slipping on the black rocks glistening in the moonlight. I saw him all at once standing at the lip of the falls. I began to shiver in the damp cold, the mist stinging my face, moonlight on the water when I heard that bear-sounding cry and he was shaking up there at the top of the falls, silver like a salmon shaking, and that cry louder than the falls for a moment, and then swallowed and he was in the air, turning over and over, moonlight finding the silver-white of his sides and dark green back before he cut into the water, the sound lost in the roar.

I did not want to leave. Sunrise. I went up onto the willow flats where I could see the sky. I felt the sunlight going deep into my hair. Good fall day. Good day to go look for chinqua-pin nuts, but I sat down and fell asleep.

When I awoke it was late. I went back to my truck and drove home. On the way I was wondering if I felt strong enough to eat salmon.

WITHIN BIRDS' HEARING

WITHIN BIRDS' HEARING

I AM ENFEEBLED BY this torrent of light. Each afternoon seems the last for me. Hammered by the sun, mapless in country but vaguely known, I am like a desiccated pit lying in a sand wash. Hope has become a bird's feather, glissading from the evening sky.

The journey started well enough. I left my home in the eastern Mojave twelve or fifteen days ago, making a path for the ocean. Like a sleek cougar I crossed the Lloma Hills, then the Little Sangre de Cristo Range. I climbed up out of the southernmost extension of White Shell Canyon without incident. Early on, the searing heat made me wary, brought me to consider traveling only at night. But, the night skies cast with haze and so near a new moon, it was impossible to find my way.

Today I thought it might rain. But it does not seem likely

now. It's been more difficult to locate water than I've known in the past, and that lack in this light and heat has added to my anxiety. Also, my grasp of how far I still have to travel is imperfect. This most of all fills me with dread.

In the distance, the stony, cactus–strewn land falls down into the drainage of the Curandera. I will turn north here this morning and hope to be in the wet canyon of the Oso by nightfall and down off this high blistered plain. From there, however far it may be, I know the river will flow to the ocean. It's comforting, each evening, to construe the ocean as my real destiny—the smooth beach underfoot, round and hard like an athlete's thigh, the ocean crashing, shaking off the wind, surging up the beach slope, all of it like wild horses. But, walking the Oso, I could come upon some sign that might direct me elsewhere, perhaps north into the Rose Peaks, into country I do not know at all.

Part of the difficulty of this journey has been having to feel my way like this. I departed—my body deft, taut—with a clear image of where I should go: the route, the dangers, the distances by day. But then the landscape became vast. Thinking too much on the end, I sometimes kept a pace poorly matched to the country. By evening I was winded, irritated, dry hearted.

I would scrape out a place on the ground and fall asleep, too exhausted to eat. My clothing, thin and worn, began to disintegrate. I would awaken dreamless, my tongue swollen from thirst, and look about delirious for any companion—a dog, a horse, another human being just waking up. But there was no one with whom to speak, no one even to offer water to. I spat my frustration out. I pushed on, resolute as Jupiter's moons, breaking down only once, weeping and licking the earth.

I did not anticipate the ways in which I would wear out.

My one salvation, a gift I can't reason through, has been the unceasing kindness of animals. Once, when I was truly lost, when the Gray Spider Hills and the Black Sparrow Hills were entirely confused in a labyrinth of memory, I saw a small coyote sitting between two creosote bushes just a few yards away. She was eyeing me quizzically, whistling me up with that look. I followed behind her without question, into country that eventually made sense to me, or which I eventually remembered.

Another time, the eighth day out, I fainted, collapsing from heat and thirst onto the cobble plain through the blood shimmer of air. I was as overwhelmed by my own foolishness, as struck down by the arrogance in my determination as I was overcome by thirst. Falling, I knew the depth of my stupidity, but not as any humiliation. I felt unshackled. Released. I came back to the surface aware of drops of water trickling into my throat. I tried to raise an arm to the harrowing sun but couldn't lift the weight. I inhaled the texture of warm silk and heard a scraping like stiffened fans. When I squinted through quivering lashes I saw I was beneath birds.

Mourning doves were perched on my chest, my head, all down my legs. Their wings flared above me like parasols. They held my lips apart with slender toes. One by one, doves settled on my cheeks. They craned their necks at angles to drip water, then flew off. Their gleaming eyes were an infant's lucid pools. Backed into this rock shelter, out of the sun's first, slanting rays, I am trying to manufacture now a desire to go on, to step once again into a light I must stroke through. The light wears like acid and the heat to come will terrorize even lizards. It is not the desert of my childhood.

I concentrate on an image of transparent water and cool air flowing through the Oso River Canyon, beyond the horizon. I will lie down naked in its current. Cool watercress will stick like rose petals to my skin. I will anoint my eyes, my fevered ears. I will lap water like a trembling dog. The fired plain before me, the wicked piercing of thorns, my knotted intestines, the lost path I will endure for that. Drawing the two together in my mind—the eviscerating heat, the forgiving water—I see the horizons of my life. My desire to arrive, to cover this distance, is so acute I whimper like a colt when I breathe.

Two days past, in Agredecido Canyon, I came upon a gallery of wild figures painted on a sheer rock escarpment a thousand years ago. I was walking on the far side of the wash and nearly missed them, concealed behind a row of tall cottonwoods. So many days in a landscape without people had made me anxious and I went quickly across, as though they were alive and could speak.

Someone's ancestors had drawn thirty-four figures on the sienna rock, many familiar and comforting—mountain sheep running, human figures traveling, and other animals free of gravity, as if they were plummeting toward the sky. Huge kachinalike demi-gods were dancing, A square-shouldered human form stood with its back turned, holding a snake. Two perplexing images attracted me. One was a series of pictographs, lined out along a cleft in the rock. The initial drawing, the one farthest to the left as I read them, was of a single bush, like sagebrush. Then came a clump of thin, thready lines, lightly incised. Then a rope coil with tattered ends and then a second rope, unwound and undulating. Lastly, a cast of double curves, like a child's seagulls flying away.

The second image was simpler, a bear tumbling on the spout of a shooting geyser. I thought it a water geyser, but the bear's large eyes and the round shape of its mouth revealed such fear that finally I believed it a geyser of blood. As with so much of what people leave behind, it's difficult to say what was meant. We can only surmise that they loved, that they were afraid.

I rise and press off. From beneath a paloverde I take a bearing on the high white disk of the sun. Looking toward the indistinct middle distance, the outwash plain of distorted mountains, I believe I am looking at the shoulder of the place where the waters of the Oso will rise.

I stride along this route just north of west, listening to the seething cut of the sickle light, feeling the black heat rise around me like water, watchful where I step. My eye is out sharply for any track, for the camouflage in which poisonous snakes hide. I find a good pace and work to hold it, adjusting breath and stride as I cross arroyos with their evidence

of flash floods and climb and descend shallow hills. I do not think of the Oso at all but only of what is around me—the powdery orange of globe mallow blossoms, lac glistening on wands of creosote bushes, bumblebees whining. The afternoon, the prostrate sky, sweep on. My feet crumble the rain pan and wind pack of dust. Breezes whisk scorched seeds toward me. The seeds, bits of brittle leaf and stem, corral my feet and lie still.

At one point I see antelope—so far south for these animals, twenty or more of them ranging to the southeast, an elongation of life under the heaved sky.

At last light, when the sun has set beneath the mountains, I am without a trace of the Oso. I sit down on a granite boulder, a slow collapse onto the bone of my haunches. The country has clearly proved more than I can imagine. I consider that I began this morning confidently, rightly seasoned I believed, and then, with every conscious fiber, I feel I will not despair. My body comes back erect with determination. I have made so many miles today. But I know—I have no good day past this one. Desperation, the heavy night tide, surges. I cannot stand again. My feet throb from stone bruises and thorn punctures. My flesh spills the shrieking heat. My tongue wads my mouth. I bow my head, my sticking eyelids, to my knees. Into this agony, as if from an unsuspected room, comes a bare cascade of sound. My wounds become silent. The long phrase descends again, a liquid tremolo. The skin over my cheekbones chills, as when sweat suddenly dries. Again the falling *tiyew, tiyew, tiyew, tiyew,* and, a turn at the end, *tew.*

I stand up to rivet the dimness. The burbling call breaks the dark once more. This time I hear each note, a canyon wren, surely, but something else. I strain my ears at the night, listening for that other sound. When it comes I realize it has been there each time, each call, an ornament hardly separated from the bird's first note. I recall vividly the last canyon wrens I heard, ones around my home where they are never far from the waters of the Colorado, their voices another purling in the dry air.

The song again, pure, sharp, now without the grace note. I fix its place and move into the night, my face averted, feeling through the darkness with my hands, sliding my feet ahead, down a scrabble slope. Long minutes pass between bursts of wren song and then there is only silence. I am standing in water for some moments before I am aware of its caress, before I can separate the pain in my feet from its soothing. A

little farther on I hear the gurgle of springs. More water, running from beneath the Sierra de San Martín. I squat down to
feel the expanse of the shallow flow. Headwaters of the Oso.

I walk a little ways, down the gathering waters.

I drink. I bathe. I rinse out my clothes.

The ocean is far away, but I feel its breath booming against
the edge of the continent. Wind evaporating water tightens
my bare flesh. I feel the running tide of my own salted blood.
In the full round air from below I can detect, though barely, a
perfume of pear blossoms and wetted fields. I can distinguish
in it the last halt cries of birds, becalmed in the marshes.

EMPIRA'S TAPESTRY

EMPIRA'S TAPESTRY

THE FALL EMPIRA LARSON came to Idora we remember not solely for her arrival but for the height of the drought. Winter rains the year before never filled the creeks. The following summer the woods were parched and brittle and we worried terribly about fire, though none came. It wasn't until Christmas that the creeks came up and the river filled.

Empira came to teach fourth grade. She boarded with me her first six months, then moved to a small house that needed repairs and was always damp, but which gave her a depth of privacy people like her seem to crave. It was my own feeling that she had arrived on the heels of some difficulty with a man—not necessarily something he had caused, either; but I didn't inquire and wouldn't have. She showed a sharp tongue if provoked but otherwise had a fine bearing and was gracious with the children. She seemed to live the life before her, not one left behind.

To be truthful, I wasn't much drawn to her at first nor did I welcome her friendship. After my husband died I felt an odd antagonism toward younger women, especially women like Empira who had made independent lives for themselves, who moved about the country freely and might have had many lovers. Empira's presence made me look poorly on my own life. In conversations with her, meal after meal, I came to know an anger that had not touched me before.

During the weeks she stayed with me I tried to regard Empira as irresponsible and self-important; but nothing in her could long sustain such a view. I held it from self-pity, I later realized. Or envy. When she moved out I missed her company so much it unnerved me. She had dispelled an atmosphere of complacency in my house, as no other boarder ever had. She was fresh as flowers. A boy staying with me briefly began to swagger around the house in such a way you could see he assumed Empira was just smitten. One night he asked her in a smug, condescending way to go to the movies. She said, "Mr. Conway, I love going to the movies, but I'm afraid I wouldn't enjoy them very much with you." She could be that blunt, but

Eldon Beemis was the single one of my long-term boarders glad to see her go. It gave him the table back, to run the supper conversation as he wished.

A year after she moved out, Empira and I and Albert Garreau, who owned the mercantile, and Deborah Purchase, another widow, were sitting in the school cafeteria after a trip with the students. We'd been out to the Pearson Prehistoric Shelter, a cave above the river east of town. It was warm. We'd gotten cool drinks. With end-of-the-day weariness we were musing about how long ago the shelter had been occupied by humans—eight thousand years, too far back for us to imagine. Albert began recounting the history of Idora, which of course seemed ephemeral by comparison. I recalled a story of my grandfather's time—he'd come to Idora in 1871 with the railroad—and that one led to another.

My grandfather's stories of Ohio and the Great Plains, and of his many trips to the Pacific and the Gulf, were ones I'd committed to memory. The language I used when I told them was different from my own. It had my grandfather's precision and force. I got caught up in his stories that day. I talked until the cafeteria was so dark I couldn't see the others' faces clearly. Albert, whom I found appealing partly because he listened to everyone so attentively, had heard many of the stories before, one following on another like a stream of water. Deborah had too. Empira's attention was rapt. When I stopped talking I felt slightly chagrined, having gone on so long with such enthusiasm. But telling the stories always had that effect on me. I felt them physically, even—Grandfather's descriptions of wind-tossed oceans of grass in Nebraska, of huge trees in the valley bottoms of western Oregon, of flocks of cranes flying over. People's desires: "... when Adrian tasted the wheat flour, the faint trace of nasturtiums was there. He bought every bag Edward Bonner had on the shelves." When I spoke of these things, it was as if I were guiding a canoe through rapids and stretches of calm water, conveying my passengers on a momentous journey down a marked but unknown path. I rose to this part of my life as I did to no other.

When Albert and then Deborah left, Empira invited me to her home for supper. I said I wasn't able to come. I wouldn't like eating in that small, dank, ramshackle house of hers. I was ashamed of myself, thinking so; and when she told me then how wondrous and strange and invigorating my stories were I felt worse. She said they were an homage to my grandfather's memory; she said that I was their custodian, and that when I told the stories I was beautiful.

My eyes filled with tears right in front of her. I couldn't help it.

Empira was a physically active woman and early on volunteered to coach girls' track at the high school, though I don't believe she knew much about it at the beginning. One Saturday morning when I was leaving for Blue River, I saw her on the cinder track behind the school and pulled over to watch her from the car. Lap after lap she ran, her cheeks red, her head bobbing, her stride too short to be graceful but relentless. I was mesmerized by her belief in herself, at the same time I questioned it.

You couldn't say what Empira cared about most. She was a good teacher, by all that I heard. Her concern for the children was genuine and tireless. She read voraciously and had a lot of music she listened to. She didn't visit much, but she carried the irksome burden of a single woman in Idora with no self-consciousness I saw. Several town men, aimless strays, foisted themselves on her. When she didn't give them what they wanted they moved on. I wondered if Empira cared at all about having a man in her life. I suspected she did, and it irritated me that she pretended it didn't. Men new to town would hear around that she was "an eccentric, selfish bitch"—that's what Albert Garreau told me when I asked. It took me a while to understand what they resented was her insistence on privacy and independence.

The third year Empira was among us she discovered she was sick. She never spoke of it directly, but I remember she came by the house one day with a book for me—we often traded mysteries—and she gave me an ebony stick at the same time. She said it was a storyteller's stick, from Ghana. The storyteller drew in the dirt with it, she said, while he spoke. I think of that as the moment she told me she was dying.

In that last year—a long summer, then the rainiest winter I can remember, a late spring—Empira began a tapestry. I'd gotten over my feelings about her house, knowing by then what lay behind them, and when I went over for supper one night I saw the loom set up on the side porch. On it was the most astonishing piece of handwork I had ever seen. An understanding swept over me then that Empira was gifted in a way I could barely comprehend. Despite her usually good manners,

Empira would deliberately annoy people on occasion if she felt they were being self-righteous––and she could be aloof. In my pettiness, I must say I enjoyed the few small barbs and comeuppances she suffered because of this. I thought they showed her limits. But when I stood in front of that tapestry my stomach dropped. I never felt the same about her again.

When I first looked at it I thought it had to be a painting, so fine was her weave. Only with my glasses on could I distinguish the threads one from another or, more amazing, the boundaries between colors. A hundred spools of thread pegged on a board ran the spectrum from plum through saffron to ruby red, with dozens of shades of blue and green and hues of brown.

The tapestry was but a quarter finished, only the left margin and most of the upper left corner done. It would be about five feet by three, a wilderness scene of bright sunlight over a canyon. A few words had been sewn in over the shadows of trees in the left foreground.

"Empira," I whispered, raising my hands in astonishment, in a kind of helplessness.

"When I was a little girl," she told me, "my parents took my brothers and me to the Grand Canyon. You can actually see all that space over the canyon, you know. I never forgot its breadth, how delicate the colors of the rocks and the sky and the trees were that hung in it. I wanted to fill that space up, to be inside it like a bird, graceful, rising, falling, flying long, winding spirals from the rim down to a landing far below."

"What are the words, here, what are they going to be?"

"What I wrote the first morning after I was married. They are my sentences of greatest desire, the purest hope I think I ever wrote." I waited for her to go on.

"I don't regret the feelings, not a word," she said, chiding me for my presumption.

"Empira, if you can weave this well, I mean with such skill, which is really so completely—"

"It's each individual thread, Marlis. Tying off each single thread. Pulling them from the spools, holding them to the light, feeling their tension, like violin strings, before they become part of the pattern."

"But it's so beautiful. And, my God, so real. You've hidden your lamp under a bushel basket."

"We suspect so little of what goes on in the world, of what is happening or has happened to us. We don't gather the threads, Marlis. We let them go and then the wind weaves

them. We let go and float. We eddy up along the river some-
where, most of us, and just wait out our time."   85

By early that summer, when classes were over, we could see
Empira was exhausted and we knew that she was ill. But none
of us, the circle of her friends—Albert, Deborah, Ellie Randall,
who was the principal, Dick Everson, who taught with her, or
Grady and Maureen Sillings, who lived next door to me—none
of us felt it right to bring it up. She had a pattern to her life that
was deliberate and private, and this was but the last part of it.

   That summer she visited each child she'd taught—of those
that still lived nearby—giving some of them books and trin-
kets. When fall came she wasn't strong enough to teach and
Ellie told her not to come in. Empira visited me regularly,
sometimes bringing flowers. She encouraged and then listened
with such pleasure to my stories. She aged in those weeks,
physically, but her temperament became more serene, and as
I listened to her speak of her own past I heard no self-pity or
recrimination. I knew then that I loved her. She finished the
tapestry but didn't tell me. I saw it at her house one morning,
still on the loom. The completed scene was brilliant, almost
luminous. The air filling the canyon was bright and depth-

less but it had the pale color she'd described. The words were unobtrusive. As I bent down to read them I was struck with an enormous sadness. "My holy and blooded desire . . . implausible as such a life can be . . . his hands tracing the bow of my back, his lips on the rim of my ear . . . bring my own children here, to find what I was given. . . ."

It rained without letup that October, not the mist and unending drizzle we are used to but downpours that flooded the air and streamed over the ground, night and day. One evening, Empira came to my door and said when I opened it, "Will you walk with me this evening, Mrs. Damien?"

I said yes, of course. We walked through the rain, down streets that led from homes on the hills to stores that fronted the highway and the park, then the river. Her stride was short, her steps firm. She spoke as we went, as her strength allowed. "You have a good memory, Marlis," she began. "Perhaps you will do me the favor of remembering all I will try to say now." I feared she would become philosophical, but she was specific, enumerating things in her house, saying to whom each was to go. A set of tattered place mats, a raw amethyst in its mother stone, a Steuben vase, a box of hummingbird feathers. Some of her choices, the beneficiaries, surprised me.

We crossed the highway and walked through the park. The muddy river, visible in the faint glow of street lamps, undulated powerfully. Empira guided us to a place where it rose to the very edge of the bank. I understood her intention in the same moment that she made a gesture with her hand to sever us. I acquiesced, against all my beliefs. She dropped her coat to the ground, pulled a shawl more tightly around her, stepped out of her shoes and moved to the river's edge. After a moment she sank down and lay over on her side. I couldn't tell then whether she moved or whether the river surged but the water rose under her and enveloped her and she was gone. Her dress crumpled last in the grip of the current and I saw that the shawl was her tapestry turned side to.

She was gone quickly, as if it hadn't happened, as if I were still listening to her voice on the hilly streets.

Two days later her body surfaced miles away in a flood eddy. I found an address for her family, a small town in eastern Pennsylvania. Her mother said there was no reason to send her back, not all that way at such expense. Could we please bury her there? she asked. We did, at the best spot Ellie and Albert and I could find at the Idora cemetery. The Reverend Arthur Thorven read an impatient service, annoyed by what he believed was a sinful act of despair, a failure of courage. It was a first funeral for most of the children. They looked on in awe, troubled, disbelieving. Some people standing there may have thought what Eldon Beemis had at breakfast that morning, opening the paper as I cleared the dishes.

"Says here Empira had cancer. Homeliness, I expect, was the root of what got her. Why she killed herself. "

I felt so sharply in that moment the poverty of my friendship.

A VISUAL MEDITATION

BARRY MOSER

AFTERWORD

AFTERWORD

EARLY IN MY WRITING LIFE I discovered a remote, desolate landscape in southeastern Oregon called the Alvord Desert. I began to visit this dry lake bed regularly, a glaring expanse of white flanked by barren mountain ranges. Being there prompted new thinking for me about the relationship between physical landscapes and descriptive language, and about the way physical setting might reinforce certain themes in a fictional narrative.

The initial story to emerge from my emotional and intellectual experience with this landscape was "Desert Notes," which I wrote when I was about twenty-four. Other stories soon followed, generally inspired by the layered geography of the Alvord and other alkali deserts in the American West. Together, these stories, which formed a kind of mosaic about such places, came to comprise *Desert Notes: Reflections in the Eye of a Raven*.

In 1974 Jim Andrews, at the time the president of Universal Press Syndicate in Kansas City, Kansas, read *Desert Notes* and said he wanted to publish the manuscript under his newly established imprint, Sheed, Andrews, & McMeel. (Earlier, in 1966, as an editor at *Ave Maria* magazine, he had published some of my first short stories.) One winter afternoon, planning to review arrangements in a contract for this book, Jim and I went for a walk in Loose Park, on the Missouri side of Kansas City. He was concerned, he told me, about my trying to make my living writing for magazines. Instead of a single-book contract for *Desert Notes*, therefore, he wanted to offer me an advance on a three-book contract. Go back to Oregon, he said, and decide what you want the other two books to be. Dumbfounded, I accepted his offer. He pulled from his overcoat pocket a letter of agreement that he had already prepared and a small check. We each signed a copy of the letter, on the gleaming black hood of his Buick Electra, and he handed me the check which, in that moment, loomed very large.

A month later I wrote Jim, telling him I intended to follow up on the broad themes and general organization of *Desert Notes* with a book called *River Notes*, later subtitled *The Dance of the Herons*. Its stories, I told him, would be set in a temperate-zone rain forest, on the banks of a white-water river in western Oregon. In keeping with our agreement I said I was also planning the third book, to be called *Animal Notes*, though I would need to figure out later how its stories would dovetail with stories in the first two books, in order to form a unified trilogy.

I had no inkling then that I would never write *Animal Notes*. The strong, if still vague, impulse behind such a book—a desire to probe the ways in which wild animals are woven into the fabric of human society—eventually became another book entirely, a work of nonfiction called *Of Wolves and Men*. In 1976, in order to fulfill the terms of our letter of agreement, I offered Jim an outline for that book, along with a set of photographs and some page layouts.

Jim published *Desert Notes* in June 1976. I finished *River Notes* a year after *Desert Notes* appeared, and it came out in the fall of 1979. A year later, in September 1980, Jim died, suddenly and unexpectedly. He was forty-four and, as far as I knew, had been in excellent health. (Around the time of the book's publication Jim had asked me, eerily, to read a particular story in *River Notes*, "Upriver," at his funeral. I couldn't manage it on the day of the funeral, but I did read the story aloud a few months later at his graveside.)

After Jim had read the outline for *Of Wolves and Men* and looked at the art and layouts, he told me he didn't have the expertise to publish the book the way he thought it should be done. He said he considered my contractual obligation to him fulfilled and urged me to take the proposal to a more capable publishing house. With his support and goodwill I submitted the book to several publishers, and in October 1978 Charles Scribner's Sons brought out *Of Wolves and Men.*

In 1980 I finished a third collection of short fiction, *Winter Count.* By then I was aware that certain of my short stories, isolated from the others, occasionally struck some readers as an experimental form of essay writing. I can understand why a reader might think this because of the extent to which I use factual detail and other "nonfictive" elements such as geographical setting. (My stories are rarely based on events in my own life, nor are they based on people I know. They're often set, however, in landscapes I've resided in or traveled through.)

In writing fiction, I've been sensitive to the peculiar authority that a presentation of fact has in our culture, of how detailed, plausible descriptions of remote geographies, for example, can create an aura of authenticity. I want that aura. Also, more than plot, I'm bent on the discovery of a pattern of association

between a character and a particular place; and, more than
establishing plot elements, I want to delineate some kind of
shift in the life of a central character. I can also understand,
then, that certain of my stories might be taken as autobiograph-
ical, especially because I regularly use first-person narrators. But
these narrators are not me.

Not all the stories I've written fit neatly inside the frame-
work I've just suggested. Some are character-driven, others
do have a minimal plot. What I'm primarily interested in, in
short fiction, is what happens to people when something outside the self—a desert landscape, an urban neighborhood, a
character the narrator encounters, weather passing through—
comes into play. (On occasion I have wondered whether what
I have actually been pursuing all these years, put simply, isn't
the nature of some buried set of profound ethical relation-
ships between a person and various components of the physical landscapes in which that person finds himself or herself.)

On that winter afternoon in Loose Park in 1975, Jim
Andrews made it possible for me to follow a path that otherwise would have been much more difficult to navigate. In the
1980s and '90s, while other books were coming along—*Arctic
Dreams, Crossing Open Ground, Crow and Weasel*—I continued to feel

an unfulfilled obligation to Jim, and to myself, to write a third book of stories that would complete the fictional trilogy we had originally agreed to.

Following a long stretch of writing essays, I returned to writing short fiction in the early 1990s. In 1993 I chose a few stories from those I'd already completed, wrote several more in a related vein, and arranged them together in a collection of twelve (to match the number I'd established in the other two books), including again, for the third time, a story entitled "Introduction." In September 1994 Knopf published *Field Notes: The Grace Note of the Canyon Wren*, what I considered the final volume in the trilogy. The stories in the first two books had been unified by their particular geographical settings; the stories in *Field Notes* were related, instead, by the numinous nature of the landscapes in which they were set.

As I see it, the same handful of questions I possessed about the meaning of human life when I was a young writer have remained with me. These concerns, about personal identity, for example, or the ethereal dimensions of reality, are now, I hope, simply more nuanced, more informed.

When I write a story, I am not trying to make a point or demonstrate any particular proficiency as a writer. I am trying to make the patterns of American cultural life more apparent, patterns any individual reader might be able to take further, metaphorically, than I am able to, patterns that I hope will serve the reader's own search for meaning. In the creation of the story, it is the reader's welfare, not the life of the writer, that is finally central.

Published by Trinity University Press

San Antonio, Texas 78212

Text copyright © 2014 by Barry Holstun Lopez

Illustrations copyright © 2014 by Barry Moser

Introduction copyright © 2014 by James Perrin Warren

These stories originally appeared in *Desert Notes: Reflections in the Eye of a Raven,*
River Notes: The Dance of Herons, and *Field Notes: The Grace Note of the Canyon Wren.*

All rights reserved. No part of this book may be reproduced in any form or by
any electronic or mechanical means, including information storage and retrieval
systems, without permission in writing from the publisher.

Trinity University Press strives to produce its books using methods and
materials in an environmentally sensitive manner. We favor working with
manufacturers that practice sustainable management of all natural resources,
produce paper using recycled stock, and manage forests with the best possible
practices for people, biodiversity, and sustainability. The press is a member
of the Green Press Initiative, a nonprofit program dedicated to supporting
publishers in their efforts to reduce their impacts on endangered forests, climate
change, and forest-dependent communities.

The paper used in this publication meets the minimum requirements of the
American National Standard for Information Sciences–Permanence of Paper for
Printed Library Materials, ansi 39.48-1992.

978-1-59534-319-2 paperback

978-1-59534-188-4 ebook

CIP data on file at the Library of Congress

29 28 27 26 25   5 4 3 2 1

OUTSIDE

*was originally published in a limited
edition of fifty copies by David Pascoe at
Nawakum Press in Santa Rosa, California.
The design and engravings are by Barry
Moser. The brush calligraphy is by Judythe
Seick of Santa Fe, New Mexico. The
typeface is Nofret, designed by Gudrun
Zapf-von Hesse, released by the H. Berthold
Type Foundry of Berlin, Germany, in 1984.*

The cover design for this trade edition of
Outside *is by Barry Moser.*

BARRY LOPEZ is the author of *Resistance, About This Life, Light Action in the Caribbean, Arctic Dreams*, for which he received the National Book Award, and nine other works of fiction and nonfiction. He is the coeditor, with Debra Gwartney, of *Home Ground: A Guide to the American Landscape*, published by Trinity University Press. He has written for a wide range of magazines, including *Harper's, Granta*, the *Paris Review*, the *Georgia Review, National Geographic*, and *Outside*, and he is a recipient of the John Burroughs Medal, the Award in Literature from the Academy of Arts and Letters, Pushcart Prizes in fiction and nonfiction, and fellowships from the Guggenheim, Lannan, and National Science Foundations. For more information, please go to www.barrylopez.com.

BARRY MOSER is the prizewinning illustrator and designer of more than 300 books for children and adults. He has won numerous accolades for his work, including the prestigious National Book Award for Design and Illustration and the Boston Globe–Horn Book Award. He is widely celebrated for his dramatic wood engravings for the only twentieth-century edition of the entire King James Bible illustrated by a single artist. His work is represented in collections throughout the world, including the Metropolitan Museum of Art, the British Museum, and the Library of Congress. Moser is the Irwin and Pauline Alper Glass Professor of Art at Smith College and serves as printer to the college. He lives in western Massachusetts.

JAMES PERRIN WARREN is the S. Blount Mason, Jr. Professor of English at Washington and Lee University. His books include *John Burroughs and the Place of Nature, Culture of Eloquence: Oratory and Reform in Antebellum America,* and *Walt Whitman's Language Experiment.*

www.ingramcontent.com/pod-product-compliance
Lightning Source LLC
Jackson TN
JSHW072332260125
77358JS00001B/1